100TH ANNIVERSARY
"All the News
That's Fit to Print"
1851   1951

The New Y

Copyright, 1951, by Th

VOL. CI.No. 34,221.

Entered as Second-Class Matter.
Post Office, New York, N. Y.

NEW YORK, THUR

GIANTS CAPTURE PENNANT, BEATING DODGERS 5-4 IN 9TH ON THOMSON'S 3-RUN HOMER

MEET YANKS TODAY

Third Baseman's Clout Sends Giants Into the World Series

BROOKLYN'S BRANCA LOSER

Yields Homer on Second Pitch After Relieving Newcombe in the Play-Off Final

By JOHN DREBINGER

In an electrifying finish to what long will be remembered as the most thrilling pennant campaign in history, Leo Durocher and his astounding never-say-die Giants wrenched victory from the jaws of defeat at the Polo Grounds yesterday, vanquishing the Dodgers, 5 to 4, with a four-run splurge in the last half of the ninth.

A three-run homer by Bobby Thomson that accounted for the final three tallies blasted the Dodgers right out of the world series picture and this afternoon at the Stadium it will be the Giants against Casey Stengel's American League champion Yankees in the opening clash of the world series.

Seemingly hopelessly beaten, 4 to 1, as the third and deciding game of the epic National League play-off moved into the last inning, the Giants lashed back with a fury that would not be denied. They routed big Don Newcombe while scoring one run.

Then, with Ralph Branca on the mound and two runners aboard the

AFTER THE GAME WAS OVER

Bobby Thomson and Manager Leo Durocher of the Giants in the clubhouse after the victory over the Dodgers. *Associated Press*

It's Like a Wake in Brooklyn As Fans 'Replay' Fatal 9th

All Gotham was divided yesterday into three parts. The first of these the lordly Yankees inhabit; the second is the joyful country of the Giants; the third belongs to the fiercest and most desperate of all, the Brooklyn Dodgers.

When Bobby Thomson exploded

GEN. HUGH A. DRUM

NEW CHIEF ORDE INQUIRY ON INCOM OF U.S. TAX OFFICIA

Dunlap Starts an Investiga of Returns, Including A Enforcement Officers

TRUMAN APPROVAL CIT

Examination Stems From T Questionnaires Issued f the New York Area

By CLAYTON KNOWLE
Special to THE NEW YORK TIMES.

WASHINGTON, Oct. 3—Joh Dunlap, Commissioner of Inte Revenue, revealed today tha had ordered a thorough exam tion of the income tax return 1948, 1949 and 1950 of all offi and front-line enforcement off of the bureau.

In reporting the order, Oct. 1, the commissioner, ju month on the job, told the and Means subcommittee of House of Representatives in gating recurring irregularitie the agency, that he had rece "carte blanche authority to things up" from both Pres Truman and John W. Snyder, retary of the Treasury.

The order stated that the e nation of returns would be "whether or not the informatio the return indicates that an e nation is warranted" and tha turns for earlier years woul requisitioned if the current revealed the need.

Continuing Check Ordere

Returns for all coming year be examined automatically. rights reserved for any taxp including the right to appeal, ployes under the order.

For the purposes of the o officials are defined on a broad enough to include ever from a division head to the missioner himself.

Front-line enforcement empl

ork Times.

w York Times Company.

AY, OCTOBER 4, 1951.

Times Square, New York 18, N. Y.
Telephone LAckawanna 4-1000

LATE CITY EDITION
Cloudy, windy today and tonight.
Possibly clearing tomorrow.
Temperature Range Today—Max., 74; Min., 64
Temperatures Yesterday—Max., 72; Min., 64
Full U. S. Weather Bureau Report, Page 67

RAG PAPER EDITION
SEVENTY-FIVE CENTS

N. UNITS ADVANCE A 40-MILE FRONT; UCE SHIFT UPSET

S., British, Greek, Filipino, th Korean, Turkish Units ollow Up Heavy Barrage

MY COUNTER-ATTACKS

Artillery Also Opens Up, but s to Halt Push—Red Reply ars Move From Kaesong

eds Reject Truce Shift
By The United Press.
OKYO, Thursday, Oct. 4—
Communist High Command
ay rejected Gen. Ridgway's
posal to change the site of
Korean truce negotiations.

Special to THE NEW YORK TIMES.
OKYO, Thursday, Oct. 4—A
sive United Nations offensive
ed off at dawn yesterday in
ral and Western Korea
nst an estimated quarter-mil-
Communist troops.
e allied attacking force com-
d elements of five divisions
ining men of nine nations—
ricans, Britons, Australians,
Zealanders, Canadians, Fili-
, Greeks, Turks and South
ans. They stepped off after a
y barrage.
e front where the battle is
raging stretches forty miles
eastward from near Korang-
within twelve miles of Kae-
, the erstwhile truce-talk city.
United Nations liaison of-
rs flew to Panmunjom and
ived a message from the
munist High Command.
aking a seven-day silence by
Communists, it was presum-
an answer to Gen. Matthew
Ridgway's request of Sept. 27
cease-fire talks be resumed,
shifted from Kaesong.]
g British Tanks in Action
South Korean First Division
s gained their immediate ob-
ve on the extreme west of the
line by early afternoon.

SOVIET'S SECOND ATOM BLAST IN 2 YEARS REVEALED BY U. S.; DETAILS ARE KEPT A SECRET

ANSWERING CHARGES BY M'CARTHY

Dr. Philip C. Jessup, Ambassador at Large, before a Senate Foreign Relations subcommittee yesterday. *The New York Times*

Jessup Denies Any Red Ties, Calls McCarthy Charge False

By WILLIAM S. WHITE
Special to THE NEW YORK TIMES.

WASHINGTON, Oct. 3—Ambassador at Large Philip C. Jessup produced documentary evidence today to show that he followed an isolationist position in World War II long after the Communists had reversed themselves and had come out for aid to the Allies.
Under oath he denounced as false, in general and in every de-
tail, the accusations of Senator Jo-
seph R. McCarthy, Republican of

BRITISH EVACUATE STAFF FROM IRAN

SPEED HERE URGED

White House Says Event Discounts Peace Aims Voiced by Stalin

STRESSES SECURITY ANGLE

Time and Place of Explosion Are Withheld—Capital Is Surprised by Report

By W. H. LAWRENCE
Special to THE NEW YORK TIMES.

WASHINGTON, Oct. 3—Soviet scientists and military men suc-
ceeded recently in exploding "an-
other atomic bomb" inside the Soviet Union, the White House an-
nounced today. All details on the location and scope of the blast were ordered withheld on the ground that disclosure of the information would affect adversely United States security interest.
News of the atomic experiment was made public by Joseph Short, White House Press Secretary, who declared that the event belied per-
sistent Communist propaganda, led personally by Premier Stalin, that the atomic energy development of the Soviet Union was being devoted exclusively to peaceful pur-
poses and not to the manufacture of weapons.
The White House statement said flatly that the latest explosion was "another atomic bomb" and thus was much more precise than was President Truman's announcement Sept. 23, 1949 of the first Russian blast. At that time Mr. Truman reported that "we have

Also by Don DeLillo

NOVELS

Americana

End Zone

Great Jones Street

Ratner's Star

Players

Running Dog

The Names

White Noise

Libra

Mao II

Underworld

The Body Artist

PLAYS

The Day Room

Valparaiso

Don DeLillo

PAFKO AT THE WALL

a novella

SCRIBNER
New York   London   Toronto   Sydney   Singapore

SCRIBNER
1230 Avenue of the Americas
New York, NY 10020

SCRIBNER and design are trademarks
of Macmillan Library Reference USA, Inc., used under license
by Simon & Schuster, the publisher of this work.

For information regarding special discounts for bulk purchases,
please contact Simon & Schuster Special Sales
at 1-800-456-6798 or *business@simonandschuster.com*

DESIGNED BY ERICH HOBBING

Manufactured in the United States of America

1   3   5   7   9   10   8   6   4   2

Library of Congress Cataloging-in-Publication Data is available.

ISBN 0-7432-3000-0

PAFKO AT THE WALL

He speaks in your voice, American, and there's a shine in his eye that's halfway hopeful.

It's a school day, sure, but he's nowhere near the classroom. He wants to be here instead, standing in the shadow of this old rust-hulk of a structure, and it's hard to blame him—this metropolis of steel and concrete and flaky paint and cropped grass and enormous Chesterfield packs aslant on the scoreboards, a couple of cigarettes jutting from each.

Longing on a large scale is what makes history. This is just a kid with a local yearning but he is part of an assembling crowd, anonymous thousands off the buses and trains, people in narrow columns tramping over the swing bridge above the river, and even if they are not a migration or a revolution, some vast shaking of the soul, they bring with them the body heat of a great city and their own small reveries and desperations, the unseen something that haunts the day—men in fedoras and sailors on shore leave, the stray tumble of their thoughts, going to a game.

The sky is low and gray, the roily gray of sliding surf.

He stands at the curbstone with the others. He is the youngest, at fourteen, and you know he's flat broke by the edgy leaning look he hangs on his body. He has never done this before and he doesn't know any of the others and only two or three of them seem to know each other but they can't do this thing singly or in pairs so they have found one another by means of slidy looks that detect the fellow foolhard and here they stand, black kids and white kids up from the subways or off the local Harlem streets, lean shadows, bandidos, fifteen in all, and according to topical legend maybe four will get through for every one that's caught.

They are waiting nervously for the ticket holders to clear the turnstiles, the last loose cluster of fans, the stragglers and loiterers. They watch the late-arriving taxis from downtown and the brilliantined men stepping dapper to the windows, policy bankers and supper club swells and Broadway hotshots, high aura'd, picking lint off their mohair sleeves. They stand at the curb and watch without seeming to look, wearing the sourish air of corner hangabouts. All the hubbub has died down, the pregame babble and swirl, vendors working the jammed sidewalks waving scorecards and pennants and calling out in ancient singsong, scraggy men hustling buttons and caps, all dispersed now, gone to their roomlets in the beaten streets.

They are at the curbstone, waiting. Their eyes are going grim, sending out less light. Somebody takes his hands out of his pockets. They are waiting and then they go, one of them goes, a mick who shouts *Geronimo*.

There are four turnstiles just beyond the pair of ticket booths. The youngest boy is also the scrawniest, Cotter Martin by name, scrawny tall in a polo shirt and dungarees and trying not to feel doom-struck—he's located near the tail of the rush, running and shouting with the others. You shout because it makes you brave or you want to announce your recklessness. They have made their faces into scream masks, tight-eyed, with stretchable mouths, and they are running hard, trying to funnel themselves through the lanes between the booths, and they bump hips and elbows and keep the shout going. The faces of the ticket sellers hang behind the windows like onions on strings.

Cotter sees the first jumpers go over the bars. Two of them jostle in the air and come down twisted and asprawl. A ticket taker puts a headlock on one of them and his cap comes loose and skims down his back and he reaches for it with a blind swipe and at the same time—everything's at the same time—he eyes the other hurdlers to keep from getting stepped on. They are running and hurdling. It's a witless form of flight with bodies packed in close and the gate-crashing becoming real. They are jumping too soon or too late and hitting the posts and radial bars, doing cartoon climbs up each other's back, and what kind of stupes must they look like to people at the hot dog stand on the other side of the turnstiles, what kind of awful screwups—a line of mostly men beginning to glance this way, jaws working at the sweaty meat and grease bubbles flurrying on their tongues, the gent at the far end going dead-still except for a hand that produces automatic movement, swabbing on mustard with a brush.

The shout of the motley boys comes banging off the deep concrete.

Cotter thinks he sees a path to the turnstile on the right. He drains himself of everything he does not need to make the jump. Some are still jumping, some are thinking about it, some need a haircut, some have girlfriends in woolly sweaters and the rest have landed in the ruck and are trying to get up and scatter. A couple of stadium cops are rumbling down the ramp. Cotter sheds these elements as they appear, sheds a thousand waves of information hitting on his skin. His gaze is trained on the iron bars projected from the post. He picks up speed and seems to lose his gangliness, the slouchy funk of hormones and unbelonging and all the stammering things that seal his adolescence. He is just a running boy, a half-seen figure from the streets, but the way running reveals some clue to being, the way a runner bares himself to consciousness, this is how the dark-skinned kid seems to open to the world, how the bloodrush of a dozen strides brings him into eloquence.

Then he leaves his feet and is in the air, feeling sleek and unmussed and sort of businesslike, flying in from Kansas City with a briefcase full of bank drafts. His head is tucked, his left leg is clearing the bars. And in one prolonged and aloof and discontinuous instant he sees precisely where he'll land and which way he'll run and even though he knows they will be after him the second he touches ground, even though he'll be in danger for the next several hours—watching left and right—there is less fear in him now.

He comes down lightly and goes easy-gaiting past the ticket taker groping for his fallen cap and he knows absolutely—knows it all the way, deep as knowing goes, he feels the knowledge start to hammer in his runner's heart—that he is uncatchable.

Here comes a cop in municipal bulk with a gun and cuffs and a flashlight and a billy club all jigging on his belt and a summons pad wadded in his pocket. Cotter gives him a juke step that sends him nearly to his knees and the hot dog eaters bend from the waist to watch the kid veer away in soft acceleration, showing the cop a little finger-wag bye-bye.

He surprises himself this way every so often, doing some gaudy thing that whistles up out of unsuspected whim.

He runs up a shadowed ramp and into a crossweave of girders and pillars and spilling light. He hears the crescendoing last chords of the national anthem and sees the great open horseshoe of the grandstand and that unfolding vision of the grass that always seems to mean he has stepped outside his life—the rubbed shine that sweeps and bends from the raked dirt of the infield out to the high green fences. It is the excitement of a revealed thing. He runs at quarter speed craning to see the rows of seats, looking for an inconspicuous wedge behind a pillar. He cuts into an aisle in section 35 and walks down into the heat and smell of the massed fans, he walks into the smoke that hangs from the underside of the second deck, he hears the talk, he enters the deep buzz, he hears the warm-up pitches crack into the catcher's mitt, a series of reports that carry a comet's tail of secondary sound.

Then you lose him in the crowd.

•　　•　　•

In the radio booth they're talking about the crowd. Looks like thirty-five thousand and how do you figure it. When you think about the textured histories of the teams and the faith and passion of the fans and the way these forces are entwined citywide, and when you think about the game itself, live-or-die, the third game in a three-game playoff, and you say the names Giants and Dodgers, and you calculate the way the players hate each other openly, and you recall the kind of year this has turned out to be, the pennant race that has brought the city to a strangulated rapture, an end-shudder requiring a German loanword to put across the mingling of pleasure and dread and suspense, and when you think about the blood loyalty, this is what they're saying in the booth—the love-of-team that runs across the boroughs and through the snuggled suburbs and out into the apple counties and the raw north, then how do you explain twenty thousand empty seats?

The engineer says, "All day it looks like rain. It affects the mood. People say the hell with it."

The producer is hanging a blanket across the booth to separate the crew from the guys who've just arrived from KMOX in St. Louis. Have to double up since there's nowhere else to put them.

He says to the engineer, "Don't forget. There wasn't any advance sale."

And the engineer says, "Plus the Giants lost big yesterday and this is a serious thing because a crushing defeat puts a gloom on the neighborhoods. Believe me, I know this where I live. It's demoralizing for people. It's like they're dying in the tens of thousands."

Russ Hodges, who broadcasts the games for WMCA, he is the voice of the Giants—Russ has an overworked larynx and the makings of a major cold and he shouldn't be lighting up a cigarette but here he goes, saying, "That's all well and good but I'm not sure there really is a logical explanation. When you deal with crowds, nothing's predictable."

Russ is going jowly now but there are elements of the uncomplicated boy in his eyes and smile and in the hair that looks bowl-cut and the shapeless suit that might belong to almost anyone. Can you do games, can you do play-by-play almost every day through a deep summer and not be located in some version of the past?

He looks out at the field with its cramped corners and the overcompensating spaces of the deep alleys and dead center. The big square Longines clock that juts up from the clubhouse. Strokes of color all around, a frescoing of hats and faces and the green grandstand and tawny base paths. Russ feels lucky to be here. Day of days and he's doing the game and it's happening at the Polo Grounds—a name he loves, a precious echo of things and times before the century went to war. He thinks everybody who's here ought to feel lucky because something big's in the works, something's building. Okay, maybe just his temperature. But he finds himself thinking of the time his father took him to see Dempsey fight Willard in Toledo and what a thing that was, what a measure of the awesome, the Fourth of July and a hundred and ten degrees and a crowd of shirtsleeved men in straw hats, many wearing handkerchiefs spread beneath their hats and down to their shoulders, making them look like play-Arabs, and the greatness of the beating big Jess took in that white hot ring, the way the sweat and blood came misting off his face every time Dempsey hit him.

When you see a thing like that, a thing that becomes a newsreel, you begin to feel you are a carrier of some solemn scrap of history.

In the second inning Thomson hits a slider on a line over third.

Lockman swings into an arc as he races toward second, looking out at left field.

Pafko moves to the wall to play the carom.

People stand in both decks in left, leaning out from the rows up front, and some of them are tossing paper over the edge, torn-up scorecards and bits of matchbook covers, there are crushed paper cups, little waxy napkins they got with their hot dogs, there are germ-bearing tissues many days old that were matted at the bottoms of deep pockets, all coming down around Pafko.

Thomson is loping along, he is striding nicely around first, leaning into his run.

Pafko throws smartly to Cox.

Thomson moves head-down toward second, coasting in, and then sees Lockman standing on the bag looking at him semi-spellbound, the trace of a query hanging on his lips.

Days of iron skies and all the mike time of the past week, the sore throat, the coughing, Russ is feverish and bedraggled—train trips and nerves and no sleep and he describes the play in his familiar homey ramble, the grits-and-tater voice that's a little scratchy today.

Cox peers out from under his cap and snaps the ball sidearm to Robinson.

Look at Mays meanwhile strolling to the plate dragging the barrel of his bat on the ground.

Robinson takes the throw and makes a spin move toward Thomson, who is standing shyly maybe five feet from second.

People like to see the paper fall at Pafko's feet, maybe drift across his shoulder or cling to his cap. The wall is nearly seventeen feet high so he is well out of range of the longest leaning touch and they have to be content to bathe him in their paper.

Look at Durocher on the dugout steps, manager of the Giants, hard-rock Leo, the gashouse scrapper, a face straight from the Gallic Wars, and he says into his fist, "Holy fuggin shit almighty."

Near the Giants' dugout four men are watching from Leo's own choice box when Robinson slaps the tag on Thomson. They are three-quarters show biz, Frank Sinatra, Jackie Gleason and Toots Shor, drinking buddies from way back, and they're accompanied by a well-dressed man with a bulldog mug, one J. Edgar Hoover. What's the nation's number one G-man doing with these crumbums? Well, Edgar is sitting in the aisle seat and he seems to be doing just fine, smiling at the rude banter that rolls nonstop from crooner to jokesmith to saloonkeeper and back. He would rather be at the racetrack but is cheerful enough in this kind of company whatever the venue. He likes to be around movie idols and celebrity athletes, around gossipmeisters such as Walter Winchell, who is also at the game today, sitting with the Dodger brass. Fame and secrecy are the high and low ends of the same fascination, the static crackle of some libidinous thing in the world, and Edgar responds to people who have access to this energy. He wants to be their dearly devoted friend provided their hidden lives are in his private files, all the rumors collected and indexed, the shadow facts made real.

Gleason says, "I told you chumps, it's all Dodgers today. I feel it in my Brooklyn bones."

"What bones?" says Frank. "They're rotted out by booze."

Thomson's whole body sags, it loses vigor and resistance, and Robinson calls time and walks the ball to the mound in the pigeon-toed gait that makes his path seem crooked.

"The Giants'll have to hire that midget if they want to win, what's-his-name, because their only hope is some freak of nature," Gleason says. "An earthquake or a midget. And since this ain't California, you better pray for an elf in flannels."

Frank says, "Fun-nee."

The subject makes Edgar nervous. He is sensitive about his height even though he is safely in the middle range. He has added weight in recent years and when he sees himself in the mirror getting dressed, thick-bodied and Buddha-headed, it is a short round man that looks back at him. And this is something the yammerheads in the press have reported to be true, as if a man can wish his phantom torment into public print. And today it's a fact that taller-than-average agents are not likely to be assigned to headquarters. And it's a further fact that the midget his pal Gleason is talking about, the three-foot seven-inch *sportif* who came to bat one time for the St. Louis Browns some six weeks ago in a stunt that was also an act, Edgar believes, of political subversion—this fellow is called Eddie Gaedel and if Gleason recalls the name he will flash-pair Eddie with Edgar and then the short-man jokes will begin to fly like the storied shit that hits the fan. Gleason got his start doing insult comedy and never really stopped—does it for free, does it for fun and leaves shattered lives behind.

Toots Shor says, "Don't be a shlump all your life, Gleason. It's only one-zip. The Giants didn't come from thirteen and a half games back just to blow it on the last day. This is the miracle year. Nobody has a vocabulary for what happened this year."

The slab face and meatcutter's hands. You look at Toots and see a speakeasy vet, dense of body, with slicked-back hair and a set of chinky eyes that summon up a warning in a hurry. This is an ex-bouncer who throws innocent people out of his club when he is drinking.

He says, "Mays is the man."

And Frank says, "This is Willie's day. He's due to bust loose. Leo told me on the phone."

Gleason does a passable clipped Britisher saying, "You're not actually telling me that this fellow stepping up to the wicket is going to do something extraordinary."

Edgar, who hates the English, falls forward laughing even as Jackie takes a breathless bite of his hot dog and begins to cough and choke, sending quidbits of meat and bread in many directions, pellets and smithereens, spitball flybys.

But it is the unseeable life-forms that dismay Edgar

most and he faces away from Gleason and holds his breath. He wants to hurry to a lavatory, a zinc-lined room with a bar of untouched oval soap, a torrent of hot water and a swansdown towel that has never been used by anyone else. But of course there is nothing of the kind nearby. Just more germs, an all-pervading medium of pathogens, microbes, floating colonies of spirochetes that fuse and separate and elongate and spiral and engulf, whole trainloads of matter that people cough forth, rudimentary and deadly.

The crowd, the constant noise, the breath and hum, a basso rumble building now and then, the genderness of what they share in their experience of the game, how a man will scratch his wrist or shape a line of swearwords. And the lapping of applause that dies down quickly and is never enough. They are waiting to be carried on the sound of rally chant and rhythmic handclap, the set forms and repetitions. This is the power they keep in reserve for the right time. It is the thing that will make something happen, change the structure of the game and get them leaping to their feet, flying up together in a free thunder that shakes the place crazy.

Sinatra saying, "Jack, I thought I told you to stay in the car until you're all done eating."

Mays takes a mellow cut but gets under the ball, sending a routine fly into the low October day. The sound of the ash bat making contact with the ball reaches Cotter Martin in the left-field stands, where he sits in a bony-shouldered hunch. He is watching Willie instead of the ball, seeing him sort of shrug-run around first and then scoop his glove off the turf and jog out to his position.

The arc lights come on, catching Cotter by surprise, causing a shift in the way he feels, in the freshness of his escapade, the airy flash of doing it and not getting caught. The day is different now, grave and threatened, rain-hurried, and he watches Mays standing in center field looking banty in all that space, completely kid-size, and he wonders how the guy can make those throws he makes, whirl and sling, with power. He likes looking at the field under lights even if he has to worry about rain and even if it's only afternoon and the full effect is not the same as in a night game when the field and the players seem completely separate from the night around them. He has been to one night game in his life, coming down from the bluff with his oldest brother and walking into a bowl of painted light. He thought there was an unknown energy flaring down out of the light towers, some intenser working of the earth, and it isolated the players and the grass and the chalk-rolled lines from anything he'd ever seen or imagined. They had the glow of first-time things.

The way the runner skid-brakes when he makes the turn at first.

The empty seats were Cotter's first surprise, well before the lights. On his prowl through the stands he kept seeing blank seats, too many to be explained by people buying a beer or taking a leak, and he found a spot between a couple of guys in suits and it's all he can do to accept his good luck, the ease of an actual seat, without worrying why there's so many.

The man to his left says, "How about some peanuts hey?"

Peanut vendor's coming through again, a coin-catching wiz about eighteen, black and rangy. People know him from games past and innings gone and they quicken up and dig for change. They're calling out for peanuts, *hey, here, bag,* and tossing coins with thumb flicks and discus arcs and the vendor's hands seem to inhale the flying metal. He is magnet-skinned, circus-catching dimes on the wing and then sailing peanut bags into people's chests. It's a thrill-a-minute show but Cotter feels an obscure danger here. The guy is making him visible, shaming him in his prowler's den. Isn't it strange how their common color jumps the space between them? Nobody saw Cotter until the vendor appeared, black rays phasing from his hands. One popular Negro and crowd pleaser. One shifty kid trying not to be noticed.

The man says, "What do you say?"

Cotter raises a hand no.

"Care for a bag? Come on."

Cotter leans away, the hand going to his midsection to mean he's already eaten or peanuts give him cramps or his mother told him not to fill up on trashy food that will ruin his dinner.

The man says, "Who's your team then?"

"Giants."

"What a year hey?"

"This weather, I don't know, it's bad to be trailing."

The man looks at the sky. He's about forty, close-shaved and Brylcreemed but with a casual quality, a free-and-easy manner that Cotter links to small-town life in the movies.

"Only down a run. They'll come back. The kind of year it's been, it can't end with a little weather. How about a soda?"

Men passing in and out of the toilets, men zipping their flies as they turn from the trough and other men approaching the long receptacle, thinking where they want to stand and next to whom and not next to whom, and the old ballpark's reek and mold are consolidated here, generational tides of beer and shit and cigarettes and peanut shells and disinfectants and pisses in the untold millions, and they are thinking in the ordinary way that helps a person glide through a life, thinking thoughts unconnected to events, the dusty hum of who you are, men shouldering through the traffic in the men's room as the game goes on, the coming and going, the lifting out of dicks and the meditative pissing.

Man to his left shifts in the seat and speaks to Cotter from off his shoulder, using a crafty whisper. "What about school? Having a private holiday?" Letting a grin slide across his face.

Cotter says, "Same as you," and gets a gunshot laugh.

"I'd a broken out of prison to see this game. Matter of fact they're broadcasting to prisoners. They put radios in cell blocks in the city jails."

"I was here early," Cotter says. "I could have gone to school in the morning and then cut out. But I wanted to see everything."

"A real fan. Music to my ears."

"See the people showing up. The players going in the players' entrance."

"My name's Bill Waterson by the way. And I'd a gladly gone AWOL from the office but I didn't actually have to. Got my own little business. Construction firm."

Cotter tries to think of something to say.

"We're the people that build the houses that are fun to live in."

Peanut vendor's on his way up the aisle and headed over to the next section when he spots Cotter and drops a knowing smile. The kid thinks here comes trouble. This gatemouth is out to expose him in some withering way. Their glances briefly meet as the vendor moves up the stairs. In full stride and double-quick he dips his hand for a bag of peanuts and zings it nonchalant to Cotter, who makes the grab in a one-hand blur that matches the hazy outline of the toss. And it is one sweetheart of a moment, making Cotter crack the smile of the week and sending a wave of goodwill through the area.

"Guess you got one after all," says Bill Waterson.

Cotter unrolls the pleated top of the brown bag and extends it to Bill. They sit there shelling the peanuts and rubbing off the tissuey brown skin with a rolling motion of thumb and index finger and eating the oily salty flesh and dropping the husks on the ground without ever taking their eyes off the game.

Bill says, "Next time you hear someone say they're in seventh heaven, think of this."

"All we need is some runs."

He pushes the bag at Bill once more.

"They'll score. It's coming. Don't worry. We'll make you happy you skipped school."

Look at Robinson at the edge of the outfield grass watching the hitter step in and thinking idly, Another one of Leo's country-boy krauts.

"Now there's a law of manly conduct," Bill says. "And it states that since you're sharing your peanuts with me, I'm duty-bound to buy us both some soda pop."

"That sounds fair enough."

"Good. It's settled then." Turning in his seat and

flinging up an arm. "A couple of sportsmen taking their ease."

Stanky the pug sitting in the dugout.

Mays trying to get a jingle out of his head, his bluesy face slightly puffed, some catchy tune he's been hearing on the radio lately.

The batboy comes down the steps a little daydreamy, sliding Dark's black bat into the rack.

The game turns inward in the middle innings. They fall into waiting, into some unshaped anxiety that stiffens the shoulder muscles and sends them to the watercooler to drink and spit.

Across the field Branca is up in the Dodger bullpen, a large man with pointy elfin ears, tight-armed and throwing easily, just getting loose.

Mays thinking helplessly, Push-pull click-click, change blades that quick.

In the stands Special Agent Rafferty is walking down the stairs to the box-seat area behind the home team dugout. He is a thickset man with a mass of reddish hair—a shock of red hair, people like to say—and he is moving with the straight-ahead look of someone who doesn't want to be distracted. He is moving briskly but not urgently, headed toward the box occupied by the Director.

Gleason has two sudsy cups planted at his feet and there's a hot dog he has forgotten about that's bulging out at each end of his squeezed fist. He is talking to six people at once and they are laughing and asking questions, season box holders, old-line fans with their spindly wives. They see he is half swacked and they admire the clarity of his wit, the fine edge of insult and derision. They want to be offended and Jackie's happy to do it, bypassing his own boozy state to do a detailed imitation of a drunk. He goes heavy-lidded and growly, making sport of one man's ragmop toupee, ridiculing a second for the elbow patches on his tweed jacket. The women enjoy it enormously and they want more. They watch Gleason, they look at Sinatra for his reaction to Gleason, they watch the game, they listen to Jackie do running lines from his TV show, they watch the mustard slide down his thumb and feel too shy to tell him.

When Rafferty reaches Mr. Hoover's aisle seat he does not stand over the Director and lean down to address him. He makes it a point to crouch in the aisle. His hand is set casually near his mouth so that no one else can make out what he is saying. Hoover listens for a moment. He says something to his companions. Then he and Rafferty walk up the stairs and find an isolated spot midway down a long ramp, where the special agent recites the details of his message.

It seems the Soviet Union has conducted an atomic test at a secret location somewhere inside its own borders. They have exploded a bomb in plain unpretending language. And our detection devices indicate this is clearly what it is—it is a bomb, a weapon, it is an instrument of conflict, it produces heat and blast and shock. It is not some peaceful use of atomic energy with home-heating applications. It is a red bomb that spouts a great white cloud like some thunder god of ancient Eurasia.

Edgar fixes today's date in his mind. October 3, 1951. He registers the date. He stamps the date.

He knows this is not completely unexpected. It is their second atomic explosion. But the news is hard, it works into him, makes him think of the spies who passed the secrets, the prospect of warheads being sent to communist forces in Korea. He feels them moving ever closer, catching up, overtaking. It works into him, changes him physically as he stands there, drawing the skin tighter across his face, sealing his gaze.

Rafferty is standing on the part of the ramp that is downhill from Mr. Hoover.

Yes, Edgar fixes the date. He thinks of Pearl Harbor, just under ten years ago, he was in New York that day as well, and the news seemed to shimmer in the air, everything in photoflash, plain objects hot and charged.

The crowd noise breaks above them, a chambered voice rolling through the hollows in the underbody of the stadium.

Now this, he thinks. The sun's own heat that swallows cities.

Gleason isn't even supposed to be here. There's a rehearsal going on right now at a midtown studio and that's where he's supposed to be, preparing a skit called "The Honeymooners," to be shown for the first time in exactly two days. This is material that's close to Jackie's heart, involving a bus driver named Ralph Kramden who lives with his wife Alice in a shabby Brooklyn flat. Gleason sees nothing strange about missing a rehearsal to entertain fans in the stands. But it's making Sinatra uneasy, all these people lapping at their seat backs. He is used to ritual distances. He wants to encounter people in circumstances laid out beforehand. Frank doesn't have his dago secret service with him today. And even with Jackie on one flank and Toots on the other—a couple of porkos who function as natural barriers—people keep pressing in, showing a sense of mission. He sees them decide one by one that they must speak to him. The rigid grins floating near. And the way they use him as a reference for everything that happens. Somebody makes a nice play, they look at Frank to see how he reacts. The beer vendor trips on a step, they look at Frank to see if he has noticed.

He leans over and says, "Jack, it's a great boot being here but you think you can put a towel over your face so these people can go back to watching the game?"

People want Gleason to do familiar lines of dialogue from the show. They're calling out the lines they want him to do.

Then Frank says, "Where the hell is Hoover by the way? We need him to keep these women off our beautiful bodies."

The catcher works up out of his squat, dirt impacted in the creases that run across the back of his ruddled neck. He lifts his mask so he can spit. He is padded and bumpered, lips rough and scored and sun-flaked. This is the freest thing he does, spitting in public. His saliva bunches and wobbles when it hits the dirt, going sandy brown.

Russ Hodges is over on the TV side for the middle innings, talking less, guided by the action on the monitor. Between innings the statistician offers him part of a chicken sandwich he has brought along for lunch.

He says to Russ, "What's the wistful look today?"

"I didn't know I had a look. Any look. I don't feel capable of a look. Maybe hollow-eyed."

"Pensive," says the statman.

And it's true and he knows it, Russ is wistful and drifting and this is so damn odd, the mood he's been in all day, a tilting back, an old creaky easing back, as of a gray-haired man in a rocker.

"This is chicken with what?"

"I'm guessing mayonnaise."

"It's funny, you know," Russ says, "but I think it was Charlotte put the look in my face."

"The lady or the city?"

"Definitely the city. I spent years in a studio doing re-creations of big league games. The telegraph bug clacking in the background and blabbermouth Hodges inventing ninety-nine percent of the action. And I'll tell you something scout's honor. I know this sounds far-fetched but I used to sit there and dream of doing real baseball from a booth in the Polo Grounds in New York."

"Real baseball."

"The thing that happens in the sun."

Somebody hands you a piece of paper filled with letters and numbers and you have to make a ball game out of it. You create the weather, flesh out the players, you make them sweat and grouse and hitch up their pants, and it is remarkable, thinks Russ, how much earthly disturbance, how much summer and dust the mind can manage to order up from a single Latin letter lying flat.

"That's not a bush curve Maglie's throwing," he says into the mike.

When he was doing ghost games he liked to take the action into the stands, inventing a kid chasing a foul ball, a carrot-topped boy with a cowlick (shameless, ain't I) who retrieves the ball and holds it aloft, this five-ounce sphere of cork, rubber, yarn, horsehide and spiral stitching, a souvenir baseball, a priceless thing somehow, a thing that seems to recapitulate the whole history of the game every time it is thrown or hit or touched.

He puts the last bite of sandwich in his mouth and licks his thumb and remembers where he is, far from the windowless room with the telegraph operator and the Morse-coded messages.

Over on the radio side the producer's saying, "See that thing in the paper last week about Einstein?"

Engineer says, "What Einstein?"

"Albert, with the hair. Some reporter asked him to figure out the mathematics of the pennant race. You know, one team wins so many of their remaining games, the other teams wins this number or that number. What are the myriad possibilities? Who's got the edge?"

"The hell does he know?"

"Apparently not much. He picked the Dodgers to eliminate the Giants last Friday."

The engineer talks through the blanket to his counterpart from KMOX. The novelty of the blanket has these men talking to each other in prison slang. When they switch to black dialect the producer gets them to stop but after a while they're at it again, doing a couple of reefer Negroes in the fumy murmurs of some cellar room. Not loud enough to be picked up on mike of course. An ambient noise like random dugout buzz—a patter, a texture, an extension of the game.

Down in the field boxes they want Gleason to say, "You're a dan-dan-dandy crowd."

Russ makes his way back to the radio side after the Giants go down in their half of the sixth still trailing by a run. He's glad he doesn't have a thermometer because he might be tempted to use it and that would be demoralizing. It's a mild day, glory be, and the rain's holding off.

Producer says, "Going to the wire, Russ."

"I hope I don't close down. My larynx feels like it's in a vise."

"This is radio, buddy. Can't close down. Think of what's out there. They are hugging their little portables."

"You're not making me feel any better."

"They are goddamn crouched over the wireless. You're like Murrow from London."

"Thank you, Al."

"Save the voice."

"I am trying mightily."

"This game is everywhere. Dow Jones tickers are rapping out the score with the stock averages. Every bar in town, I guarantee. They're smuggling radios into boardrooms. At Schrafft's I hear they're breaking into the Muzak to give the score."

"All those nice ladies with their matched sweater sets and genteel sandwiches."

"Save the voice," Al says.

"Do they have tea with honey on the menu?"

"They're eating and drinking baseball. The track announcer at Belmont's doing updates between races. They got it in taxicabs and barbershops and doctors' offices."

They're all waiting on the pitcher, he's a faceful of boding, upper body drawn forward, glove hand dangled at the knee. He's reading and reading the sign. He's reading the sign. Hitter fidgeting in the box. This son of a buck can bring it.

The shortstop moves his feet to break the trance of waiting.

It's the rule of confrontation, faithfully maintained, written across the face of every slackwit pitcher since there were teams named the Superbas and the Bridegrooms. The difference comes when the ball is hit. Then nothing is the same. The men are moving, coming out of their crouches, and everything submits to the pebble-skip of the ball, to rotations and backspins and airstreams. There are drag coefficients. There are trailing vortices. There are things that apply unrepeatably, muscle memory and pumping blood and jots of dust, the narrative that lives in the spaces of the official play-by-play.

And the crowd is also in this lost space, the crowd made over in that one-thousandth of a second when the bat and the baseball are in contact. A rustle of murmurs and curses, people breathing soft moans, their faces changing as the play unrolls across the grassy scan. John

Edgar Hoover stands among them. He is watching from the wide aisle at the head of the ramp. He has told Rafferty he will remain at the game. No purpose served by his leaving. The White House will make the announcement in less than an hour. Edgar hates Harry Truman, he would like to see him writhing on a parquet floor, felled by chest pains, but he can hardly fault the President's timing. By announcing first, we prevent the Soviets from putting their own sweet spin on the event. And we ease public anxiety to some degree. People will understand that we've maintained control of the news if not of the bomb. This is no small subject of concern. Edgar looks at the faces around him, open and hopeful. He wants to feel a compatriot's nearness and affinity. All these people formed by language and climate and popular songs and breakfast foods and the jokes they tell and the cars they drive have never had anything in common so much as this, that they are sitting in the furrow of destruction. He tries to feel a belonging, an opening of his old stopcocked soul. But there is some bitter condition he has never been able to name and when he encounters a threat from outside, from the moral wane that is everywhere in effect, he finds it is a balance to this state, a restoring force. His ulcer kicks up of course. But there is that side of him, that part of him that depends on the strength of the enemy.

Look at the man in the bleachers who's pacing the

aisles, a neighborhood crazy, he waves his arms and mumbles, short, chunky, bushy-haired—could be one of the Ritz Brothers or a lost member of the Three Stooges, the Fourth Stooge, called Flippo or Dummy or Shaky or Jakey, and he's distracting the people nearby, they're yelling at him to siddown, goway, meshuggener, and he paces and worries, he shakes his head and moans as if he knows something's coming, or came, or went—he's receptive to things that escape the shrewdest fan.

It is a stone-faced Director who returns to his seat for the seventh-inning stretch. He says nothing of course. Gleason is shouting down a vendor, trying to order beers. People on their feet, shaking off the tension and fret. A man slowly wiping his glasses. A staring man. A man flexing the stiffness out of his limbs.

"Get me a brandy and soda," Toots says.

Jackie tells him, "Don't be a clamhead all your life."

"Treat the man nice," Frank says. "He's come a long way for a Jew who drinks. He's best buddies with world leaders you never even heard of. They all roll into his joint sooner or later and knock back a brandy with Toots. Except maybe Mahatma Gandhi. And *him* they shot."

Gleason flares his brows and goggles his eyes and shoots out his arms in a nitwit gesture of revelation.

"That's the name I couldn't think of. The midget that pinch-hits."

People around them, hearing part of this and reacting

mainly to inflection and gesture—they've seen Jackie physically building the remark and they knock together laughing even before he has finished the line.

Edgar is also laughing despite the return of the midget business. He admires the rough assurance of these men. It seems to flush from their pores. They have a size to them, a natural stamina that mocks his own bible-school indoctrination even as it draws him to the noise. He's a self-perfected American who must respect the saga of the knockabout boy emerging from a tenement culture, from backstreets slant with danger. It makes for gusty egos, it makes for appetites. The pussy bandits Jackie and Frank have a showy sort of ease around women. And it's true about Toots, he knows everybody worth knowing and can drink even Gleason into the carpeting. And when he clamps a sympathetic paw on your shoulder you feel he is some provident force come to guide you out of old despond.

Frank says, "This is our inning."

And Toots says, "Better be. Because these shit-heel Dodgers are making me nervous."

Jackie is passing beers along the row.

Frank says, "Seems to me we've all made our true loyalties known. Shown our hearts' desire. We got a couple of old-timey Giant fans. And this porpoise with a haircut from Brooklyn. But what about our friend the G-man. Is it G for Giants? Fess up, Jedgar. Who's your team?"

J. Edgar. Frank calls him Jedgar sometimes and the Director likes the name although he never lets on—it is medieval and princely and wily-dark.

A faint smile creeps across Hoover's face.

"I don't have a rooting interest. Whoever wins," he says softly. "That's my team."

He is thinking of something else entirely. The way our allies one by one will receive the news of the Soviet bomb. The thought is grimly cheering. Over the years he has found it necessary to form joint ventures with the intelligence heads of a number of countries and he wants them all to die a little.

Look at the four of them. Each with a hanky neatly tucked in his breast pocket. Each holding his beer away from his body, leaning forward to tease the high scud from the rim of the cup. Gleason with a flower in his lapel, a damp aster snatched from a vase at Toots' place. People are still after him to do lines from the show.

They want him to say, "Harty har-har."

The plate umpire stands mask in hand, nearly blimp-ish in his outfitting. He is keeping the numbers, count-ing the pitcher's warm-up tosses. This is the small dogged conscience of the game. Even in repose he shows a history thick with embranglement, dust-stomping men turning figures in the steep sun. You can see it in his face, chin thrust out, a glower working under his brow. When the number reaches eight he aims a spurt from his chaw and prepares to take his whiskbroom to the rubber slab.

In the stands Bill Waterson takes off his jacket and dangles it lengthwise by the collar. It is rippled and mauled and seems to strike him as a living body he might want to lecture sternly. After a pause he folds it over twice and drops it on his seat. Cotter is sitting again, surrounded by mostly vertical people. Bill looms above him, a sizable guy, a one-time athlete by the look of him, getting thick in the middle, his shirt wet under the arms. Lucky seventh. Cotter needs a measly run to keep him from despairing—the cheapest eked-out unearned run ever pushed across. Or he's ready to give up. You know that thing that happens when you give up before the end and then your team comes back to perform acts of valor and you feel a queasy shame stealing over you like pond slick.

Bill says down to him, "I take my seventh-inning stretch seriously. I not only stand. I damn well make it a point to stretch."

"I've been noticing," says Cotter.

"Because it's a custom that's been handed down. It's part of something. It's our own little traditional thing. You stand, you stretch—it's a privilege in a way."

Bill has some fun doing various stylized stretches, the bodybuilder, the pet cat, and he tries to get Cotter to do a drowsy kid in a classroom.

"Did you ever tell me your name?"

"Cotter."

"That's the thing about baseball, Cotter. You do what they did before you. That's the connection you make. There's a whole long line. A man takes his kid to a game and thirty years later this is what they talk about when the poor old mutt's wasting away in the hospital."

Bill scoops his jacket off the seat and puts it on his lap when he sits down. Seconds later he is standing again, he and Cotter watching Pafko chase down a double. A soft roar goes up, bushy and dense, and the fans send more paper sailing to the base of the wall. Old shopping lists and ticket stubs and wads of fisted newsprint come falling around Pafko in the faded afternoon. Farther out in left field they are dropping paper on the Dodger bullpen, on the working figure of Labine and the working figure of Branca and the two men who are catching them and the men sitting under the canted roof that juts from the wall, the gum-chewing men with nothing to say.

Branca wears the number thirteen blazoned on his back.

"Told you," Bill says. "What did I tell you? I told you. We're coming back."

"We still have to score the run," Cotter says.

They take their seats and watch the hitter steer a look right up the line at Durocher dummying through the signs from the coach's box at third. Then Bill is on his feet again, rolling up his sleeves and shouting encouragement to the players, common words of spark and heart.

Cotter likes this man's singleness of purpose, his insistence on faith and trust. It's the only force available against the power of doubt. He figures he's in the middle of getting himself befriended. It's a feeling that comes from Bill's easy voice and his sociable sweaty gymnasium bulk and the way he listens when Cotter speaks and the way he can make Cotter believe this is a long and close association they share—boon companions goes the saying. He feels a little strange, it's an unfamiliar thing, talking to Bill, but there's a sense of something protective and enclosing that will help him absorb the loss if it should come to that.

Lockman squares around to bunt.

There's a man in the upper deck leafing through a copy of the current issue of Life. There's a man on 12th Street in Brooklyn who has attached a tape machine to his radio so he can record the voice of Russ Hodges broadcasting the game. The man doesn't know why he's doing this. It is just an impulse, a fancy, it is like hearing the game twice, it is like being young and being old, and this will turn out to be the only known recording of Russ' famous account of the final moments of the game. The game and its extensions. The woman cooking cabbage. The man who wishes he could be done with drink.

They are the game's remoter soul. Connected by the pulsing voice on the radio, joined to the word-of-mouth that passes the score along the street and to the fans who call the special phone number and the crowd at the ballpark that becomes the picture on television, people the size of minute rice, and the game as rumor and conjecture and inner history. There's a sixteen-year-old in the Bronx who takes his radio up to the roof of his building so he can listen alone, a Dodger fan slouched in the gloaming, and he hears the account of the mis-played bunt and the fly ball that scores the tying run and he looks out over the rooftops, the tar beaches with their clotheslines and pigeon coops and splatted con-doms, and he gets the cold creeps. The game doesn't change the way you sleep or wash your face or chew your food. It changes nothing but your life.

The producer says, "At last, at least, a run."

Russ is frazzled, brother, he is raw and rumpled and uncombed. When the teams go to the top of the eighth he reports that they have played one hundred and fifty-four regular season games and two play-off games and seven full innings of the third play-off game and here they are tied in a knot, absolutely deadlocked, they are stalemated, folks, so light up a Chesterfield and stay right here.

•　　•　　•

The next half inning seems to take a week. Cotter sees the Dodgers put men on first and third. He watches Maglie bounce a curve in the dirt. He sees Cox bang a shot past third. A hollow clamor begins to rise from the crowd, men calling from the deep reaches, an animal awe and desolation.

In the booth Russ sees the crowd begin to lose its coherence, people sitting scattered on the hard steps, a priest with a passel of boys filing up the aisle, paper rolling and skittering in the wind. He hears the announcer from St. Louis on the other side of the blanket, it is Harry Caray and he sounds like his usual chipper self and Russ thinks of the Japanese term for ritual disembowelment and figures he and Harry ought to switch names about now.

Light washing from the sky, Dodgers scoring runs, a man dancing down the aisle, a goateed black in a Bing Crosby shirt. Everything is changing shape, becoming something else.

Cotter can barely get out the words.

"What good does it do to tie the score if you're going to turn around and let them walk all over you?"

Bill says, "They're going into that dugout and I guarantee you they're not giving up. There's no quit in this team. Don't pull a long face on me, Cotter. We're buddies in bad times—gotta stick together."

Cotter feels a mood coming on, a complicated self-pity, the strength going out of his arms and a voice commencing in his head that reproaches him for caring. And the awful part is that he wallows in it. He knows how to find the twisty compensation in this business of losing, being a loser, drawing it out, expanding it, making it sickly sweet, being someone carefully chosen for the role.

The score is 4–1.

It should have rained in the third or fourth inning. Great rain drenching down. It should have thundered and lightning'd.

Bill says, "I'm still a believer. What about you?"

The pitcher takes off his cap and rubs his forearm across his hairline. Big Newk. Then he blows in the cap. Then he shakes the cap and puts it back on.

Shor looks at Gleason.

"Still making with the mouth. Leave the people alone already. They came here to see a game."

"What game? It's a lambasting. We ought to go home."

"We're not going home," Toots says.

Jackie says, "We can beat the crowd, clamhead."

Frank says, "Let's take a vote."

Toots says, "You're tubercular in the face. Sit back and watch the game. Because nobody goes until I go and I ain't going."

Jackie waves down a vendor and orders beer all

around. Nothing happens in the home half of the eighth. People are moving toward the exit ramps. It is Erskine and Branca in the bullpen now with the odd paper shaving dropped from the upper deck. Dodgers go down in the top of the ninth and this is when you sense a helpless scattering, it is tastable in the air, audible in the lone-wolf calls from high in the stands. Nothing you've put into this is recoverable and you don't know whether you want to leave at once or stay forever, living under a blanket in the wind.

Engineer says, "Nice season, boys. Let's do it again sometime."

The closeness in the booth, all this crammed male-ness is making Russ a little edgy. He lights another cigarette and for the first time all day he does not reproach himself for it. He hears the solitary wailing, he hears his statistician reciting numbers in fake French. It is all part of the same thing, the feeling of some collapsible fact that's folded up and put away, and the school gloom that traces back for decades—the last laden day of summer vacation when the range of play tapers to a screw-turn. This is the day he has never shaken off, the final Sunday before the first Monday of school. It carried some queer deep shadow out to the western edge of the afternoon.

He wants to go home and watch his daughter ride her bike down a leafy street.

Dark reaches for a pitch and hits a seeing-eye bouncer that ticks off the end of the first baseman's glove.

A head pops up over the blanket, it's the engineer from KMOX and he starts telling a joke about the fastest lover in Mexico—*een Mayheeko*. An amazing chap named Speedy Gonzalez.

Russ is thinking base hit all the way but glances routinely at the clubhouse sign in straightaway center to see if the first E in CHESTERFIELD lights up, indicating error.

Robinson retrieves the ball in short right.

"So this guy's on his honeymoon in Acapulco and he's heard all the stories about the incredible cunning of Speedy Gonzalez and he's frankly worried, he's a highly nervous type and so on the first night, the night of nights, he's in bed with his wife and he's got his middle finger plugged up her snatch to keep Speedy Gonzalez from sneaking in there when he's not looking."

Mueller stands in, taking the first pitch low.

In the Dodger dugout a coach picks up the phone and calls the bullpen for the eighteenth time to find out who's throwing good and who ain't.

Mueller sees a fastball belt-high and pokes a single to right.

"So then he's dying for a smoke and he reaches over for a second to get his cigarettes and matches."

Russ describes Dark going into third standing up. He

sees Thomson standing in the dugout with his arms raised and his hands held backwards gripping the edge of the roof. He describes people standing in the aisles and others moving down toward the field.

Irvin dropping the weighted bat.

"So then he lights up quick and reaches back to the bed finger-first."

Maglie's already in the clubhouse sitting in his skivvies in that postgame state of disrepair and pit stink that might pass for some shambles of the inner man, slugging beer from the bottle.

Irvin stands in.

Russ describes Newcombe taking a deep breath and stretching his arms over his head. He describes Newcombe looking in for the sign.

"And Speedy Gonzalez says, Sen-yor-or, you got your finger up my a-ass."

Russ hears most of this and wishes he hadn't. He does a small joke of his own, half standing to drape the mike with his suit coat as if to keep the smallest syllable of raunchy talk from reaching his audience. Decent people out there.

Fastball high and away.

The crowd noise is uncertain. They don't know if this is a rally in the works or just another drag-tail finish that draws out the pain. It's a high rackety noise that makes Russ think of restive waiting in a train station.

Irvin tries to pull it, overeager, and Russ hears the soul of the crowd repeat the sorry arc of the baseball, a moaned vowel falling softly to earth. First baseman puts it away.

Decent people out there. Russ wants to believe they are still assembled in some recognizable manner, the kindred unit at the radio, old lines and ties and propinquities.

Lockman stands in, the towhead from Caroline.

How his family used to gather around the gramophone and listen to grand opera, the trilled *r*'s of old Europe. These thoughts fade and return. They are not distractions. He is alert to every movement on the field.

A couple of swabbies move down to the rail near third base.

How the records were blank on one side and so brittle they would crack if you looked at them cross-eyed. That was the going joke.

He is hunched over the mike. The field seems to open outward into nouns and verbs. All he has to do is talk.

Saying, "Carl Erskine and fireballer Ralph Branca still throwing in the bullpen."

Pitch.

Lockman fouls it back into the netting.

Now the rhythmic applause starts, tentative at first, then spreading densely through the stands. This is how the crowd enters the game. The repeated three-beat has the force of some abject faith, a desperate kind of will toward magic and accident.

Lockman stands in once more, wagging the yellow bat.

How his mother used to make him gargle with warm water and salt when he complained of a sore throat.

Lockman hits the second pitch on a low line over third. Russ hears Harry Caray shouting into the mike on the other side of the blanket. Then they are both shouting and the ball is slicing toward the line and landing fair and sending up a spew of dirt and forcing Pafko into the corner once again.

Men running, the sprint from first to third, the man who scores coming in backwards so he can check the action on the base paths. All the Giants up at the front of the dugout. The crowd is up, heads weaving for better views. Men running through a slide of noise that comes heaving down on them.

The pitch was off the plate and he wrong-wayed it and Harry started shouting.

The hit obliterates the beat of the crowd's rhythmic clapping. They're coming into open roar, making a noise that keeps enlarging itself in breadth and range. This is the crowd made over, the crowd renewed.

Harry started shouting and then Pafko went into the corner and Russ started shouting and the paper began to fall.

One out, one in, two runs down, men on second and third. Russ thinks every word may be his last. He feels the redness in his throat, the pinpoint constriction. Mueller still on the ground at third, injured sliding or not sliding, stopping short and catching his spikes on the bag, a man in pain, the flare of pulled tendons.

Paper is falling again, crushed traffic tickets and field-stripped cigarettes and work from the office and score-cards in the shape of airplanes, windblown and mostly white, and Pafko walks back to his position and alters stride to kick a soda cup lightly and the gesture functions as a form of recognition, a hint of some concordant force between players and fans, the way he nudges the white cup, it's a little onside boot, completely unbegrudging—a sign of respect for the sly contrivances of the game, the patterns that are undivinable.

The trainer comes out and they put Mueller on a stretcher and take him toward the clubhouse. Mueller's pain, the pain the game exacts—a man on a stretcher makes sense here.

The halt in play has allowed the crowd to rebuild its noise. Russ keeps pausing at the mike to let the sound collect. This is a rumble of a magnitude he has never heard before. You can't call it cheering or rooting. It's a territorial roar, the claim of the ego that separates the crowd from other entities, from political rallies or prison riots—everything outside the walls.

Russ nuzzles up to the mike and tries to be calm although he is very close to speaking in a shout because this is the only way to be heard.

Men clustered on the mound and the manager waving to the bullpen and the pitcher walking in and the pitcher leaving and the runner for Mueller doing kneebends at third.

They are banging on the roof of the booth.

Russ says, "So don't go way. Light up that Chesterfield. We're gonna stay right here and see how big Ralph Branca will fare."

Yes. It is Branca coming through the dampish glow. Branca who is tall and stalwart but seems to carry his own hill and dale, he has the aura of a man encumbered. The drooping lids, leaden feet, the thick ridge across the brow. His face is set behind a somber nose, broad-bridged and looming.

The stadium police are taking up posts.

Look at the man in the upper deck. He is tearing pages out of his copy of Life and dropping them uncrumpled over the rail, letting them fall in a seesaw drift on the bawling fans below. He is moved to do this by the paper falling elsewhere, the contagion of paper—it is giddy and unformulated fun. He begins to ignore the game so he can waft pages over the rail. It brings him into contact with the other paper throwers and with the fans in the lower deck who reach for his pages and catch them—they are all a second force that runs parallel to the game.

Not far away another man feels something pulling at his chest, arms going numb. He wants to sit down but doesn't know if he can reach an arm back to lower himself to the seat. Heart, my heart, my god.

Branca who is twenty-five but makes you think he exemplifies ancient toil. By the time he reaches the mound the stretcher bearers have managed to get Mueller up the steps and into the clubhouse. The crowd forgets him. They would forget him if he were dead. The noise expands once more. Branca takes the ball and the men around the mound recede to the fringes.

Shor looks at Gleason.

He says, "Tell me you want to go home. What happened to let's go home? If we leave now, we can beat the crowd."

He says, "I can't visualize it enough, both you crumbums, you deserve every misery in the book."

Jackie looks miserable all right. He loosens his necktie and undoes the top button of his shirt. He's the only member of the quartet not on his feet but it isn't the shift in the game that has caused his discomfort. It's the daylong booze and the greasy food.

Shor says, "Tell me you want to go home so I can run ahead and hold the car door open and like *usher* you inside."

Paper is coming down around the group, big slick pages from a magazine, completely unremarkable in the uproar of the moment. Frank snatches a full-page ad for something called pasteurized process cheese food, a Borden's product, that's the company with the cow, and there's a color picture of yellowish pressed pulp melting horribly on a hot dog.

Frank deadpans the page to Gleason.

"Here. This will help you digest."

Jackie sits there like an air traveler in a downdraft. The pages keep falling. Baby food, instant coffee, encyclopedias and cars, waffle irons and shampoos and blended whiskeys. Piping times, an optimistic bounty that carries into the news pages where the nation's farmers record a bumper crop. And the resplendent products, how the dazzle of a Packard car is repeated in the feature story about the art treasures of the Prado. It is all part of the same thing. Rubens and Titian and Playtex and Motorola. And here's a picture of Sinatra himself sitting in a nightclub in Nevada with Ava Gardner and would you check that cleavage. Frank didn't know he was in this week's Life until the page fell out of the sky. He has people who are supposed to tell him these things. He keeps the page and reaches for another to stuff in Gleason's face. Here's a Budweiser ad, pal. In a country that's in a hurry to make the future, the names attached to the products are an enduring reassurance. Johnson & Johnson and Quaker State and RCA Victor and Burlington Mills and Bristol-Myers and General Motors. These are the venerated emblems of the burgeoning economy, easier to identify than the names of battlefields or dead presidents. Not that Jackie's in the mood to scan a magazine. He is sunk in deep inertia, a rancid sweat developing, his mouth filled with the foretaste of massive inner shiftings.

Branca takes the last of his warm-up tosses, flicking the glove to indicate a curve. Never mind the details of manner or appearance, the weight-bearing body at rest. Out on the mound he is strong and loose, cutting smoothly out of his windup, a man who wants the ball.

Furillo watching from right field. The stone-cut profile.

The bushy-haired man still pacing in the bleachers, moaning and shaking his head—call the men in the white suits and get him outta here. Talking to himself, head-wagging like a street-corner zealot with news of some distant affliction dragging ever closer. Siddown, shaddap, they tell him.

Frank keeps putting pages in Gleason's face.

He tells him, "Eat up, pal. Paper clears the palate."

When in steps Thomson.

The tall fleet Scot. Reminding himself as he gets set in the box. See the ball. Wait for the ball.

Russ is clutching the mike. Warm water and salt. Gargle, said his mother.

Thomson's not sure he sees things clearly. His eyeballs are humming. There's a feeling in his body, he's digging in, settling into his stance, crowd noise packing the sky, and there's a feeling that he has lost the link to his surroundings. Alone in all this rowdy-dow. See the ball. Watch and wait. He is frankly a little fuddled is Bobby. It's like the first waking moment of the day and you don't know whose house you're in.

Russ says, "Bobby Thomson up there swinging."

Mays down on one knee in the on-deck circle half leaning on his cradled bat and watching Branca go into a full windup, push-pull click-click, thinking it's all on him if Thomson fails, the season riding on him, and the jingle plays in his head, it's the radio embrace of the air itself, the mosaic of the air, and it will turn itself off when it's ready.

There's an emergency station under the stands and what the stadium cop has to do is figure out a way to get the stricken man down there without being overrun by a rampant stomping crowd. The victim looks okay considering. He is sitting down, waiting for the attendant to arrive with the wheelchair. All right, maybe he doesn't look so good. He looks pale, sick, worried and infarcted. But he can make a fist and stick out his tongue and there's not much the cop can do until the wheelchair arrives, so he might as well stand in the aisle and watch the end of the game.

Thomson in his bent stance, chin tucked, waiting.

Russ says, "One out, last of the ninth."

He says, "Branca pitches, Thomson takes a strike called on the inside corner."

He lays a heavy decibel on the word strike. He pauses to let the crowd reaction build. Do not talk against the crowd. Let the drama come from them.

Those big rich pages airing down from the upper deck.

Lockman stands near second and tries to wish a hit onto Thomson's bat. That may have been the pitch he wanted. Belt-high, a shade inside—won't see one that good again.

Russ says, "Bobby hitting at two ninety-two. He's had a single and a double and he drove in the Giants' first run with a long fly to center."

Lockman looks across the diamond at home. The double he hit is still a presence in his chest, it's chugging away in there, a body-memory that plays the moment over. He is peering into the deltoid opening between the catcher's knees. He sees the fingers dip, the blunt hand make a flapping action up and left. They'll give him the fastball high and tight and come back with the curve away. A pretty two-part scheme. Seems easy and sweet from here.

Russ says, "Brooklyn leads it four to two."

He says, "Runner down the line at third. Not taking any chances."

Thomson thinking it's all happening too fast. Thinking quick hands, see the ball, give yourself a chance.

Russ says, "Lockman without too big of a lead at second but he'll be running like the wind if Thomson hits one."

In the box seats J. Edgar Hoover plucks a magazine page off his shoulder, where the thing has lighted and stuck. At first he's annoyed that the object has come in contact with his body. Then his eyes fall upon the page. It is a color reproduction of a painting crowded with medieval figures who are dying or dead—a landscape of visionary havoc and ruin. Edgar has never seen a painting quite like this. It covers the page completely and must surely dominate the magazine. Across the red-brown earth, skeleton armies on the march. Men impaled on lances, hung from gibbets, drawn on spoked wheels fixed to the tops of bare trees, bodies open to the crows. Legions of the dead forming up behind shields made of coffin lids. Death himself astride a slat-ribbed hack, he is peaked for blood, his scythe held ready as he presses people in haunted swarms toward the entrance of some helltrap, an oddly modern construction that could be a subway tunnel or office corridor. A background of ash skies and burning ships. It is clear to Edgar that the page is from Life and he tries to work up an anger, he asks himself why a magazine called Life would want to reproduce a painting of such lurid and dreadful dimensions. But he can't take his eyes off the page.

Russ Hodges says, "Branca throws."

Gleason makes a noise that is halfway between a sigh and a moan. It is probably a sough, as of rustling surf in some palmy place. Edgar recalls the earlier blowout, Jackie's minor choking fit. He sees a deeper engagement here. He goes out into the aisle and up two steps, separating himself from the imminent discharge of animal, vegetable and mineral matter.

Not a good pitch to hit, up and in, but Thomson swings and tomahawks the ball and everybody, everybody watches. Except for Gleason who is bent over in his seat, hands locked behind his neck, a creamy strand of slime swinging from his lips.

Russ says, "There's a long drive."

His voice has a burst in it, a charge of expectation.

He says, "It's gonna be."

There's a pause all around him. Pafko racing toward the left-field corner.

He says, "I believe."

Pafko at the wall. Then he's looking up. People thinking where's the ball. The scant delay, the stay in time that lasts a hairsbreadth. And Cotter standing in section 35 watching the ball come in his direction. He feels his body turn to smoke. He loses sight of the ball when it climbs above the overhang and he thinks it will land in the upper deck. But before he can smile or shout or bash his neighbor on the arm. Before the moment can overwhelm him, the ball appears again, stitches visibly spinning, that's how near it hits, banging at an angle off a pillar—hands flashing everywhere.

Russ feels the crowd around him, a shudder passing through the stands, and then he is shouting into the mike and there is a surge of color and motion, a crash that occurs upward, stadium-wide, hands and faces and shirts, bands of rippling men, and he is outright shouting, his voice has a power he'd thought long gone—it may lift the top of his head like a cartoon rocket.

He says, *"The Giants win the pennant."*

A topspin line drive. He tomahawked the pitch and the ball had topspin and dipped into the lower deck and there is Pafko at the 315 sign looking straight up with his right arm braced at the wall and a spate of paper coming down.

He says, *"The Giants win the pennant."*

Yes, the voice is excessive with a little tickle of hysteria in the upper register. But it is mainly wham and whomp. He sees Thomson capering around first. The hat of the first-base coach—the first-base coach has flung his hat straight up. He went for a chin-high pitch and coldcocked it good. The ball started up high and then sank, missing the facade of the upper deck and dipping into the seats below—pulled in, swallowed up—and the

Dodger players stand looking, already separated from the event, staring flat into the shadows between the decks.

He says, *"The Giants win the pennant."*

The crew is whooping. They are answering the roof bangers by beating on the walls and ceiling of the booth. People climbing the dugout roofs and the crowd shaking in its own noise. Branca on the mound in his tormented slouch. He came with a fastball up, a pitch that's tailing in, and the guy's supposed to take it for a ball. Russ is shouting himself right out of his sore throat, out of every malady and pathology and complaint and all the pangs of growing up and every memory that is not tender.

He says, *"The Giants win the pennant."*

Four times. Branca turns and picks up the rosin bag and throws it down, heading toward the clubhouse now, his shoulders aligned at a slant—he begins the long dead trudge. Paper falling everywhere. Russ knows he ought to settle down and let the mike pick up the sound of the swelling bedlam around him. But he can't stop shouting, there's nothing left of him but shout.

He says, "Bobby Thomson hits into the lower deck of the left-field stands."

He says, "The Giants win the pennant and they're going crazy."

He says, "They're going crazy."

Then he raises a pure shout, wordless, a holler from the old days—it is fiddlin' time, it is mountain music on

WCKY at five-thirty in the morning. The thing comes jumping right out of him, a jubilation, it might be *heyyy-ho* or it might be *oh-boyyy* shouted backwards or it might be something else entirely—hard to tell when they don't use words. And Thomson's teammates gathering at home plate and Thomson circling the bases in gamesome leaps, buckjumping—he is forever Bobby now, a romping boy lost to time, and his breath comes so fast he doesn't know if he can handle all the air that's pouring in. He sees men in a helter-skelter line waiting at the plate to pummel him—his teammates, no better fellows in the world, and there's a look in their faces, they are stunned by a happiness that has collapsed on them, bright-eyed under their caps.

He tomahawked the pitch, he hit on top of it and now his ears are ringing and there's a numbing buzz in his hands and feet. And Robinson stands behind second, hands on hips, making sure Thomson touches every base. You can almost see brave Jack grow old.

Look at Durocher spinning. Russ pauses for the first time to catch the full impact of the noise around him. Leo spinning in the coach's box. The manager stands and spins, he is spinning with his arms spread wide— maybe it's an ascetic rapture, a thing they do in mosques in Anatolia.

People make it a point to register the time.

Edgar stands with arms crossed and a level eye on

Gleason folded over. Pages dropping all around them, it is a fairly thick issue—laxatives and antacids, sanitary napkins and corn plasters and dandruff removers. Jackie utters an aquatic bark, it is loud and crude, the hoarse call of some mammal in distress. Then the surge of flannel matter. He seems to be vomiting someone's taupe pajamas. The waste is liquidy smooth in the lingo of adland and it is splashing freely on Frank's stout oxford shoes and fine lisle hose and on the soft woven wool of his town-and-country trousers.

The clock atop the clubhouse reads 3:58.

Russ has got his face back into the mike. He shouts, "I don't believe it." He shouts, "I don't believe it." He shouts, "I do *not* believe it."

They are coming down to crowd the railings. They are coming from the far ends of the great rayed configuration and they are moving down the aisles and toward the rails.

Pafko is out of paper range by now, jogging toward the clubhouse. But the paper keeps falling. If the early paper waves were slightly hostile and mocking, and the middle waves a form of fan commonality, then this last demonstration has a softness, a selfness. It is coming down from all points, laundry tickets, envelopes swiped from the office, there are crushed cigarette packs and sticky wrap from ice-cream sandwiches, pages from memo pads and pocket calendars, they are throwing faded dollar bills, snapshots torn to pieces, ruffled paper swaddles for cupcakes, they are tearing up letters they've been carrying around for years pressed into their wallets, the residue of love affairs and college friendships, it is happy garbage now, the fans' intimate wish to be connected to the event, unendably, in the form of pocket litter, personal waste, a thing that carries a shadow identity— rolls of toilet tissue unbolting lyrically in streamers.

They are gathered at the netting behind home plate, gripping the tight mesh.

Russ is still shouting, he is not yet shouted out, he believes he has a thing that's worth repeating.

Saying, "Bobby Thomson hit a line drive into the lower deck of the left-field stands and the place is going crazy."

Next thing Cotter knows he is sidling into the aisle. The area is congested and intense and he has to pry his way row by row using elbows and shoulders. Nobody much seems to notice. The ball is back there in a mighty pileup of shirts and jackets. The game is way behind him. The crowd can have the game. He's after the baseball now and there's no time to ask himself why. They hit it in the stands, you go and get it. It's the ball they play with, the thing they rub up and scuff and sweat on. He's going up the aisle through a thousand pounding hearts. He's prodding and sideswiping. He sees people dipping frantically, it could be apple-bobbing in Indiana, only slightly violent. Then the ball comes free and someone goes after it, the first one out of the pack, a young guy in a scuttling crawl with people reaching for him, trying to grab his jacket, a fistful of trouser-ass. He has wiry reddish hair and a college jacket—you know those athletic jackets where the sleeves are one color and leathery looking and the body is a darker color and probably wool and these are the college colors of the team.

Cotter takes a guess and edges his way along a row that's two rows down from the action. He takes a guess, he anticipates, it's the way you feel something will happen and then you watch it uncannily come to pass, occurring almost in measured stages so you can see the wheelwork of your idea fitting into place.

He coldcocked the pitch and the ball shot out there and dipped and disappeared. And Thomson bounding down on home plate mobbed by his teammates, who move in shuffled steps with hands extended to keep from spiking each other. And photographers edging near and taking their spread stances and the first of the fans appearing on the field, the first strays standing wary or whirling about to see things from this perspective, astonished to find themselves at field level, or running right at Thomson all floppy and demented, milling into the wedge of players at home plate.

Frank is looking down at what has transpired. He stands there hands out, palms up, an awe of muted disgust. That this should happen here, in public, in the high revel of event—he feels a puzzled wonder that exceeds his aversion. He looks down at the back of Jackie's glossy head and he looks at his own trouser cuffs flaked an intimate beige and the spatter across his shoe tops in a strafing pattern and the gumbo puddle nearby that contains a few laggard gobs of pinkoid stuff from deep in Gleason's gastric sac.

And he nods his head and says, "My shoes."

And Shor feels offended, he feels a look come into his face that carries the sting of a bad shave, those long-ago mornings of razor pull and cold water.

And he looks at Frank and says, "Did you see the homer at least?"

"I saw part and missed part."

And Shor says, "Do I want to take the time to ask which part you missed so we can talk about it on the phone some day?"

There are people with their hands in their hair, holding in their brains.

Frank persists in looking down. He allows one foot to list to port so he can examine the side of his shoe for vomit marks. These are handcrafted shoes from a narrow street with a quaint name in oldest London.

And Shor says, "We just won unbelievable, they're ripping up the joint, I don't know whether to laugh, shit or go blind."

And Frank says, "I'm rooting for number one or number three."

Russ is still manning the microphone and has one last thing to say and barely manages to get it out.

"The Giants won it. By a score of five to four. And they're picking Bobby Thomson up. And carrying him off the field."

If his voice has an edge of disquiet it's because he has to get to the clubhouse to do interviews with players and coaches and team officials and the only way to get out there is to cross the length of the field on foot and he's already out of breath, out of words, and the crowd is growing over the walls. He sees Thomson carried by a phalanx of men, players and others, mostly others—the players have run for it, the players are dashing for the clubhouse—and he sees Thomson riding off-balance on the shoulders of men who might take him right out of the ballpark and into the streets for a block party.

Gleason is suspended in wreckage, drained and humped, and he has barely the wit to consider what the shouting's about.

The field streaked with people, the hat snatchers, the swift kids who imitate banking aircraft, their spread arms steeply raked.

Look at Cotter under a seat.

All over the city people are coming out of their houses. This is the nature of Thomson's homer. It makes people want to be in the streets, joined with others, telling others what has happened, those few who haven't heard—comparing faces and states of mind.

And Russ has a hot mike in front of him and has to find someone to take it and talk so he can get down to the field and find a way to pass intact through all that mangle.

And Cotter is under a seat handfighting someone for the baseball. He is trying to get a firmer grip. He is trying to isolate his rival's hand so he can prise the ball away finger by finger.

It is a tight little theater of hands and arms, some martial test with formal rules of grappling.

The iron seat leg cuts into his back. He hears the earnest breathing of the rival. They are working for advantage, trying to gain position.

The rival is blocked off by the seat back, he is face-down in the row above with just an arm stuck under the seat.

People make it a point to read the time on the clock atop the notched facade of the clubhouse, the high battlement—they register the time when the ball went in.

It is a small tight conflict of fingers and inches, a lifetime of effort compressed into seconds.

He gets his hands around the rival's arm just above the wrist. He is working fast, thinking fast—too much time and people take sides.

The rival, the foe, the ofay, veins stretched and bulged between white knuckles. If people take sides, does Cotter have a chance?

Two heart attacks, not one. A second man collapses on the field, a well-dressed fellow not exactly falling but letting himself down one knee at a time, slow and controlled, easing down on his right hand and tumbling dully over. No one takes this for a rollick. The man is not the type to do dog tricks in the dirt.

And Cotter's hands around the rival's arm, twisting in opposite directions, burning the skin—it's called an Indian burn, remember? One hand grinding one way, the other going the other, twisting hard, working fast.

There's a pause in the rival's breathing. He is pausing to note the pain. He fairly croons his misgivings now and Cotter feels the arm jerk and the fingers lift from the ball.

Thomson thrusting down off the shoulders of the men who carry him, beating down, pulling away from grabby hands—he sees players watching intently from the clubhouse windows.

And Cotter holds the rival's arm with one hand and goes for the ball with the other. He sees it begin to roll past the seat leg, wobbling on the textured surface. He sort of traps it with his eye and sends out a ladling hand.

The ball rolls in a minutely crooked path into the open.

The action of his hand is as old as he is. It seems he has been sending out this hand for one thing or another since the minute he shot out of infancy. Everything he knows is contained in the splayed fingers of this one bent hand.

Heart, my heart.

The whole business under the seat has taken only seconds. Now he's backing out, moving posthaste—he's got the ball, he feels it hot and buzzy in his hand.

A sense of people grudgingly getting out of his way, making way but not too quickly, dead-eye sidewalk faces.

The ball is damp with the heat and sweat of the rival's hand. Cotter's arm hangs lank at his side and he empties out his face, scareder now than he was when he went over the turnstile but determined to look cool and blank and going down the rows by stepping over seat backs and fitting himself between bodies and walking on seats when it is convenient.

Look at the ushers locking arms at the wrists and making a sedan seat for the cardiac victim and hauling him off to the station under the grandstand.

One glance back at the area above, he allows himself a glance and sees the rival getting to his feet. The man stands out, white-shirted and hulking, and it's not the college boy he thought it might be, the guy in the varsity jacket who'd been scrambling for the ball.

And the man catches his eye. This is not what Cotter

wants, this is damage to the cause. He made a mistake looking back. He allowed himself a glance, a sidewise flash, and now he's caught in the man's hard glare.

The raised seams of the ball are pulsing in his hand.

Their eyes meet in the spaces between rocking bodies, between faces that jut and the broad backs of shouting fans. Celebration all around him. But he is caught in the man's gaze and they look at each other over the crowd and through the crowd and it is Bill Waterson with his shirt stained and his hair all punished and sprung— good neighbor Bill flashing a cutthroat smile.

The dead have come to take the living. The dead in winding-sheets, the regimented dead on horseback, the skeleton that plays a hurdy-gurdy.

Edgar stands in the aisle fitting together the two facing pages of the reproduction. People are climbing over seats, calling hoarsely toward the field. He stands with the pages in his face. He hadn't realized he was seeing only half the painting until the left-hand page drifted down and he got a glimpse of rust brown terrain and a pair of skeletal men pulling on bell ropes. The page brushed against a woman's arm and spun into Edgar's godfearing breast.

Thomson is out in center field now dodging fans who come in rushes and jumps. They jump against his body, they want to take him to the ground, show him snap-shots of their families.

Edgar reads the copy block on the matching page. This is a sixteenth-century work done by a Flemish master, Pieter Bruegel, and it is called *The Triumph of Death*.

A nervy title methinks. But he is intrigued, he admits it—the left-hand page may be even better than the right.

He studies the tumbrel filled with skulls. He stands in the aisle and looks at the naked man pursued by dogs. He looks at the gaunt dog nibbling the baby in the dead woman's arms. These are long gaunt starveling hounds, they are war dogs, hell dogs, boneyard hounds beset by parasitic mites, by dog tumors and dog cancers.

Dear germ-free Edgar, the man who has an air-filtration system in his house to vaporize specks of dust—he finds a fascination in cankers, lesions and rotting bodies so long as his connection to the source is strictly pictorial.

He finds a second dead woman in the middle ground, straddled by a skeleton. The positioning is sexual, unquestionably. But is Edgar sure it's a woman bestrad-dled or could it be a man? He stands in the aisle and they're all around him cheering and he has the pages in his face. The painting has an instancy that he finds striking. Yes, the dead fall upon the living. But he begins to see that the living are sinners. The cardplayers, the lovers who dally, he sees the king in an ermine cloak with his fortune stashed in hogshead drums. The dead have come to empty out the wine gourds, to serve a skull on a platter to gentlefolk at their meal. He sees gluttony, lust and greed.

Edgar loves this stuff. Edgar, Jedgar. Admit it—you love it. It causes a bristling of his body hair. Skeletons with wispy dicks. The dead beating kettledrums. The sackcloth dead slitting a pilgrim's throat.

The meatblood colors and massed bodies, this is a census-taking of awful ways to die. He looks at the flaring sky in the deep distance out beyond the headlands on the left-hand page—Death elsewhere, Conflagration in many places, Terror universal, the crows, the ravens in silent glide, the raven perched on the white nag's rump, black and white forever, and he thinks of a lonely tower standing on the Kazakh Test Site, the tower armed with the bomb, and he can almost hear the wind blowing across the Central Asian steppes, out where the enemy lives in long coats and fur caps, speaking that old weighted language of theirs, liturgical and grave. What secret history are they writing? There is the secret of the bomb and there are the secrets that the bomb inspires, things even the Director cannot guess—a man whose own sequestered heart holds every festering secret in the Western world—because these plots are only now evolving. This is what he knows, that the genius of the bomb is printed not only in its physics of particles and rays but in the occasion it creates for new secrets. For every atmospheric blast, every glimpse we get of the bared force of nature, that weird peeled eyeball exploding over the desert—for every one of these he reckons a hundred plots go underground, to spawn and skein.

And what is the connection between Us and Them, how many bundled links do we find in the neural labyrinth? It's not enough to hate your enemy. You have to understand how the two of you bring each other to deep completion.

The old dead fucking the new. The dead raising coffins from the earth. The hillside dead tolling the old rugged bells that clang for the sins of the world.

He looks up for a moment. He takes the pages from his face—it is a wrenching effort—and looks at the people on the field. Those who are happy and dazed. Those who run around the bases calling out the score. The ones who are so excited they won't sleep tonight. Those whose team has lost. The ones who taunt the losers. The fathers who will hurry home and tell their sons what they have seen. The husbands who will surprise their wives with flowers and chocolate-covered cherries. The fans pressed together at the clubhouse steps chanting the players' names. The fans having fistfights on the subway going home. The screamers and berserkers. The old friends who meet by accident out near second base. Those who will light the city with their bliss.

· · ·

Cotter walks at a normal pace in the afterschool light. He goes past rows of tenements down Eighth Avenue with a small solemn hop in his stride, a kind of endless levered up-and-down, and Bill is positioned off his shoulder maybe thirty yards back.

He sees the Power of Prayer sign and carries the ball in his right hand and rubs it up several times and looks back and sees the college boy in the two-tone jacket fall in behind Bill, the guy who was involved in the early scuffle for the ball.

Bill has lost his buckaroo grin. He barely shows an awareness that Cotter exists, a boy who walks the earth in high-top Keds. Cotter's body wants to go. But if he starts running at this point, what we have is a black kid running in a mainly white crowd and he's being followed by a pair of irate whites yelling thief or grief or something.

They walk down the street, three secret members of some organized event.

Bill calls out, "Hey Cotter buddy come on, we won this game together."

Many people have disappeared into cars or down the subways, they are swarming across the walkway on the bridge to the Bronx, but there are still enough bodies to disrupt traffic in the streets. The mounted police are out,

high-riding and erect, appearing among the cars as levi-
tated beings.

"Hey Cotter I had my hand on that ball before you
did."

Bill says this good-natured. He laughs when he says it
and Cotter begins to like the man all over again. Car
horns are blowing all along the street, noises of joy and
mutual salute.

The college boy says, "I think it's time I got in this. I'm
in this too. I was the first one to grab ahold of the ball.
Actually long before either one of you. Somebody hit it
out of my hand. I mean if we're talking about who was
first."

Cotter is watching the college boy speak, looking back
diagonally. He sees Bill stop, so he stops. Bill is stopping
for effect. He wants to stop so he can measure the college
boy, look him up and down in an itemizing way. He is
taking in the two-tone jacket, the tight red hair, he is taking in the whole boy, the entire form and structure of the
college boy's status as a land animal with a major brain.

And he says, "What?" That's all. A hard sharp *what*.

And he stands there agape, his body gone slack in a
comic dumbness that's pervaded with danger.

He says, "Who the hell are you anyway? What are you
doing here? Do I *know* you?"

Cotter watches this, entertained by the look on the
college boy's face. The college boy thought he was part

of a team, it's us against him. Now his eyes don't know where to go.

Bill says, "This is between my buddy Cotter and me. Personal business, understand? We don't want you here. You're ruining our fun. And if I have to make it any plainer, there's going to be a family sitting down to dinner tonight minus a loved one."

Bill resumes walking and so does Cotter. He looks back to see the college boy following Bill for a number of paces, unsurely, and then falling out of step and beginning to fade down the street and into the crowd.

Bill looks at Cotter and grins narrowly. It is a wolfish sort of look with no mercy in it. He carries his suit jacket clutched and bunched in his hand, wadded up like something he might want to throw.

With advancing dark the field is taking on a deeper light. The grass is incandescent, it has a heat and sheen. People go running past, looking half ablaze, and Russ Hodges moves with the tentative steps of some tourist at a grand bazaar, trying to hand-shuffle through the crowd.

Some ushers are lifting a drunk off the first-base line and the man warps himself into a baggy mass and shakes free and begins to run around the bases in his oversized raincoat with long belt trailing.

Russ makes his way through the infield and dancesteps into an awkward jog that makes him feel ancient and extraneous and he thinks of the ballplayers of his youth, the men with redneck monickers whose endeavors he followed in the papers every day, Eppa Rixey and Hod Eller and old Ivy Wingo, and there is a silly grin pasted across his face because he is a forty-one-year-old man with a high fever and he is running across a ball field to conduct a dialogue with a pack of athletes in their underwear.

He says to someone running near him, "I don't believe it, I still don't believe it."

Out in dead center he sees the clubhouse windows catch the trigger-glint of flashbulbs going off inside. He hears a shrill cheer and turns and sees the raincoat drunk sliding into third base. Then he realizes the man running alongside is Al Edelstein, his producer.

Al shouts, "Do you believe it?"

"I do not believe it," says Russ.

They shake hands on the run.

Al says, "Look at these people." He is shouting and gesturing, waving a Cuban cigar. "It's like I-don't-know-what."

"If you don't know what, then I don't know what."

"Save the voice," says Al.

"The voice is dead and buried. It went to heaven on a sunbeam."

"I'll tell you one thing's for certain, old pal. We'll never forget today."

"Glad you're with me, buddy."

The running men shake hands again. They are deep in the outfield now and Russ feels an ache in every joint. The clubhouse windows catch the flash of the popping bulbs inside.

In the box seats across the field Edgar sets his hat at an angle on his head. It is a dark gray homburg that brings out the nicely sprinkled silver at his temples.

He has the Bruegel folded neatly in his pocket and will take these pages home to study further.

Thousands remain in the stands, not nearly ready to leave, and they watch the people on the field, aimless eddies and stirrings, single figures sprinting out of crowds. Edgar sees someone dangling from the wall in right-center field. These men who drop from the high walls like to hang for a while before letting go. They hit the ground and crumple and get up slowly. But it's the static drama of the dangled body that Edgar finds compelling, the terror of second thoughts.

Gleason is on his feet now, crapulous Jack all rosy and afloat, ready to lead his buddies up the aisle.

He rails at Frank. "Nothing personal, pal, but I wonder if you realize you're smelling up the ballpark. Talk about stinko. I can smell you even with Shor on the premises. Usually with Shor around, blind people are tapping for garbage cans in their path."

Shor thinks this is funny. Light comes into his eyes

and his face goes crinkly. He loves the insults, the slurs and taunts, and he stands there beaming with balloon-head love. It is the highest thing that can pass between men of a certain mind—the stand-up scorn that carries their affections.

But what about Frank? He says, "It's not my stink. It's your stink, pal. Just happens I am the one that's wearing it."

Says Gleason, "Hey. Don't think you're the first friend I ever puked on. I puked on better men than you. Consider yourself honored. This is a form of flattery I extend to nearest and dearest." Here he waves his cigarette. "But don't think I am riding in any limousine that has you in it."

They march toward the exit ramp with Edgar going last. He turns toward the field on an impulse and sees another body dropping from the outfield wall, a streaky length of limbs and hair and flapping sleeves. There is something apparitional in the moment and it chills and excites him and sends his hand into his pocket to touch the bleak pages hidden there.

The crowd is thinning quickly now and Cotter goes past the last of the mounted police down around 148th Street.

"Hey Cotter now let's be honest. You snatched it out

of my hand. A clear case of snatch and run. But I'm willing to be reasonable. Let's talk turkey. What do you say to ten dollars in crisp bills? That's a damn fair offer. Twelve dollars. You can buy a ball and a glove for that."

"That's what you think."

"All right, whatever it takes. Let's find a store and go in. A fielder's glove and a baseball. You got sporting goods stores around here? Hell, we won the game of our lives. There's cause for celebration."

"The ball's not for sale. Not this ball."

Bill says, "Let me tell you something, Cotter." Then he pauses and grins. "You got quite a grip, you know. My arm needs attention in a big way. You really put the squeeze on me."

"Lucky I didn't bite. I was thinking about it."

Bill seems delighted at the way Cotter has entered the spirit of the moment. The side streets are weary with uncollected garbage and broken glass, with the odd plundered car squatting flat on its axle and men who stand in doorways completely adream.

Bill runs toward Cotter, he takes four sudden running steps, heavy and overstated, arms spread wide and a movie growl rolling from his throat. Cotter sees it is a joke but not until he has run into the street and done a loop around a passing car.

They smile at each other across the traffic.

"I looked at you scrunched up in your seat and I

thought I'd found a pal. This is a baseball fan, I thought, not some delinquent in the streets. You seem to be dead set on disappointing me. Cotter? Buddies sit down together and work things out."

The streetlights are on. They are walking briskly now and Cotter isn't sure who was first to step up the pace. He feels a pain in his back where the seat leg was digging in.

"Now tell me what it's going to take to separate you from that baseball, son."

Cotter doesn't like the tone of this.

"I want that cotton-pickin' ball."

Cotter keeps walking.

"Hey goofus I'm talking to you. You maybe think this is some cheapo entertainment. String the guy along."

"You can talk all you want," Cotter says. "The ball's not yours, it's mine. I'm not selling it or trading it."

A car comes veering off the avenue and Cotter stops to let it go by. Then he feels something shift around him. There's a ripple in the pavement or the air and a scant second in a woman's face nearby—her eyes shift to catch what's happening behind him. He turns to see Bill coming wide and fast and arm-pumping. It seems awful heavy traffic for a baseball. The color coming into Bill's face, the shiny fabric at his knees. He has a look that belongs to someone else entirely, a man out of another experience, desperate and propelled.

Cotter stands there for one long beat. He wastes a head-fake, then starts to run down the empty side street with Bill right on his neck and reaching. He cuts sharp and ducks away, skidding to his knees and wheeling on his right hand, the ball hand, pressing the ball hard in the tar and using it to pivot. Bill goes past him in a drone of dense breath, a formal hum that is close to speech. Cotter sees him stop and turn. He is skewed with rage, face bloated and quirked. A sleeve hangs down from the jacket in his hand and brushes softly on the ground.

Cotter runs back up to the avenue with the sound of rustling breath behind him. They are past the ballpark crowd, this is unmixed Harlem here—all he has to do is get to the corner, to people and lights. He sees barroom neon and bedsheets strung across a lot. He sees Fresh Killed Chickens From The Farm. He reads the sign, or maybe gathers it whole, and there's an odd calm completion in it, a gesturing of safety. Two women step aside when he gets near—they glance past him to his pursuit and he notes the alertness in their faces, the tapering of attention. Bill is close, banging the asphalt in his businessman's shoes.

Cotter goes south on the avenue and runs half a block and then he turns and does a caper, he does a physical jape—running backwards for a stretch, high-stepping, mocking, showing Bill the baseball. He's a cutup in a sour state. He holds the ball chest-high and turns it in his fingers, which isn't easy when you're running—he rotates the ball on its axis, spins it slowly over and around, showing the two hundred and sixteen raised red cotton stitches.

Don't tell me you don't love this move.

The maneuver makes Bill slow down. He looks at Cotter backpedaling, doing a danceman's strut, but he doesn't detect an opening here. Because the maneuver makes him realize where he is. The fact that Cotter's not scared. The fact that he's parading the baseball. Bill stops completely but is too smart to look around. Best to limit your purview to straight ahead. Because you don't know who might be looking back at you. And the more enlightened he becomes, the more open grows the space for Cotter's anger. He doesn't really know how to show it. This is the second time today he has taunted someone but he doesn't feel the spunky rush of dodging the cop. The high heart of the gate-crash is a dimness here—he is muddled and wrung out and can't get his bad-ass glare to function. So he stands there flatfoot and looks at Bill with people walking by and noticing and not notic- ing and he spins the ball up and over the back of his hand and catches it skipping off his wrist with a dip and twist of the same hand, like fuck you mister who you messing with.

He looks at Bill, a flushed and panting man who has vainly chased along a railroad track for the five-oh-nine.

Then he turns his back and walks slowly down the street. He begins to think about the game's amazing end. What could not happen actually happened. He wants to get home, sit quiet, let it live again, let the home run roll over him, soaking his body with a kind of composure, the settled pleasure that comes after the thing itself.

A man calls from a window to a man on a stoop.

"Hey baby I hear she put your nightstick in a sling."

Cotter turns here, looks there, feeling a sense of placeness that grows more familiar.

He sees a kid he knows but doesn't stop to show him the ball or brag on the game.

He feels the pain from the seat leg.

He sees a street-corner shouter making a speech, a tall man in a rag suit with bicycle clips nipping his pants at the ankles.

He feels a little bringdown working in his mind.

He sees four guys from a local gang, the Alhambras, and he crosses the street to avoid them and then crosses back.

He gets to his street and goes up the front steps and into the sour air of his building and he feels the little bringdown of fading light that he has felt a thousand times before.

Shit man. I don't want to go to school tomorrow.

●　　●　　●

Russ Hodges stands on an equipment trunk trying to describe the scene in the clubhouse and he knows he is making no sense and the players who climb up on the trunk to talk to him are making no sense and they are all talking in unnatural voices, failed voices, creaturely night screaks. Others are pinned to their lockers by reporters and family members and club officials and they can't get to the liquor and beer located on a table in the middle of the room. Russ holds the mike over his head and lets the noise sweep in and then lowers the mike and says another senseless thing.

Thomson goes out on the clubhouse veranda to respond to the sound of his chanted name and they are everywhere, they are on the steps with stadium cops keeping them in check and there are thousands more spread dense across the space between jutting bleacher walls, many arms extended toward Thomson—they are pointing or imploring or making victory fists or stating a desire to touch, men in suits and hats down there and others hanging over the bleacher wall above Bobby, reaching down, half falling over the edge, some very near to touching him.

Al says, the producer, "Great job today, Russ buddy."

"We did something great just by being here."

"What a feeling."

"I'd smoke a cigar but I might die."

"But what a feeling," Al says.

"We sure pulled something out of a hat. All of us together. Damn I just realized."

"What's a ball game to make us feel like this?"

"I have to go back. Left my topcoat in the booth."

"We need a walk to settle us down."

"We need a long walk."

"That's the only coat you've ever loved," says Al.

They leave by way of the Dodger clubhouse and there's Branca all right, the first thing you see, stretched facedown on a flight of six steps, feet touching the floor. He's still in uniform except for shirt and cap. He wears a wet undershirt and his head is buried in his crossed arms on the top step. Al and Russ speak to a few of the men who remain. They talk quietly and try not to look at Branca. They look but tell themselves they aren't. Next to Branca a coach sits in full uniform but hatless, smoking a cigarette. His name is Cookie. No one wants to catch Cookie's eye. Al and Russ talk quietly to a few more men and all of them together try not to look at Branca.

The steps from the Dodger clubhouse are nearly clear of people. Thomson has gone back inside but there are fans still gathered in the area, waving and chanting. The two men begin to walk across the outfield and Al points to the place in the left-field stands where the ball went in.

"Mark the spot. Like where Lee surrendered to Grant or some such thing."

Russ thinks this is another kind of history. He thinks they will carry something out of here that joins them all in a rare way, that binds them to a memory with protective power. People are climbing lampposts on Amsterdam Avenue, tooting car horns in Little Italy. Isn't it possible that this midcentury moment enters the skin more lastingly than the vast shaping strategies of eminent leaders, generals steely in their sunglasses—the mapped visions that pierce our dreams? Russ wants to believe a thing like this keeps us safe in some undetermined way. This is the thing that will pulse in his brain come old age and double vision and dizzy spells—the surge sensation, the leap of people already standing, that bolt of noise and joy when the ball went in. This is the people's history and it has flesh and breath that quicken to the force of this old safe game of ours. And fans at the Polo Grounds today will be able to tell their grandchildren—they'll be the gassy old men leaning into the next century and trying to convince anyone willing to listen, pressing in with medicine breath, that they were here when it happened.

The raincoat drunk is running the bases. They see him round first, his hands paddling the air to keep him from drifting into right field. He approaches second in a burst of coattails and limbs and untied shoelaces and swinging belt. They see he is going to slide and they stop and watch him leave his feet.

All the fragments of the afternoon collect around his

airborne form. Shouts, bat-cracks, full bladders and stray yawns, the sand-grain manyness of things that can't be counted.

It is all falling indelibly into the past.

Praise for Underworld

"A masterpiece in which the depth and reach of the commonplace are invested with universal scope and grandeur. *Underworld* is also a thrilling page-turner."
—David Wiegand,
The San Francisco Chronicle Book Review

"The most powerful and original novel by one of the strongest American writers of our time."
—Peter Wolfe, *St. Louis Post-Dispatch*

"Courageous, ingenious, and demanding, *Underworld* is a book to be talked about . . . for years to come."
—Tom LeClair, *The Atlantic Monthly*

"*Underworld*'s intellect, its view, its fabulous drama, its soul, its passion and compassion, and the beauty of the writing, just the size and generosity of it, are all of some spectacular high order."
—Michael Herr, author of *Dispatches*

"The larger the canvas, the better DeLillo paints. He is a novelist of big themes. . . . *Underworld* is a tour de force."
—Geoffrey Norman, *Playboy*

"DeLillo's most affecting novel yet . . . a dazzling, phosphorescent work of art."

—Michiko Kakutani, *The New York Times*

"*Underworld* soars. Bigger and richer than anything Don DeLillo has done before, this multicharacter, time-leaping, sea-to-shining-sea dissection of Cold War American life is perilously good—so good, so strong, deep, knowing and funny, that you might be tempted to read it and it alone, fanatically, the rest of your days."

—Phil Hanrahan, *Milwaukee Journal Sentinel*

"Anyone who wants to try to understand and appreciate the last half-century of life in these United States can do no better than read Don DeLillo's magnificent, beautifully written, and outrageously persuasive new novel, *Underworld*, unquestionably his masterpiece. . . . A triumphant performance."

—Sam Coale, *Providence Journal-Bulletin*